JaNey
Just in case

Written by Mandy Woolf

Illustrated by Elmira Georgieva

In memory of
Debra Jane

Janey's head was always full of worries.

She tried hard to push them aside, but they always came back.

Her biggest worry of all was tomorrow...
her first day of school!

That night, she tossed and turned;
waking early to pack her bag, adding
a few extras, just in case.

Two pencil cases...

...a torch,

two packets of plasters,

tissues,

Plasters

10 pack

a cardigan

her favourite dolly,

a teddy

goggles

and some wellie boots!

At breakfast, she couldn't decide what to eat.

Daddy's eggs smelt yummy;
Sophie's cereal looked good;
Mummy's toast made her
mouth melt.

In the end she asked
for everything,
just in case.

Janey looked at her breakfast and...

Her tummy felt fluttery, her hands were sticky, her head was spinning.

She couldn't eat anything!

"Let's pack your snack instead," whispered Daddy.

But Janey couldn't decide on one snack.

So in the end, she took some extras, just in case.

Ten boxes of raisins,
a small juice, a cup,
two napkins, two apples
and two oranges!

"Wow, this is heavy! Maybe we should take a few extras out?" asked Daddy.

Janey's eyes filled with tears. "But I need everything… just in case!"

Daddy lifted Janey's backpack onto his shoulder and clasping her hand they set off for school.

"Are you sure you want your bag to be this full, Janey?" he asked.

"I do Daddy... just in case."

Janey looked around at her new classmates.

A boy next to her was searching through his backpack, frantically pulling everything out.

His eyes finally rested on Janey as he squeezed, pushed and pulled at his fidget ball.

Janey's hand reached towards him as a tiny voice escaped from her.

"Hello."

The boy looked up.
"I can't find my pencil case."

"I have a spare one… just in case,"
Janey whispered and offered it to the boy.

"Oh! Thank you. My name's Ben,"
he replied, holding the pencil case
tightly in his hands.

A girl near her sat quietly,
hot prickly tears sliding down
her cheeks.

Janey dug deep into her backpack,
pulled out her dolly and some tissues,
then offered them to girl.

"Thank you. My name's Sadie,"
the girl said, holding out her
hand to Janey.

Janey held her own teddy
and clutched Sadie's hand tightly.

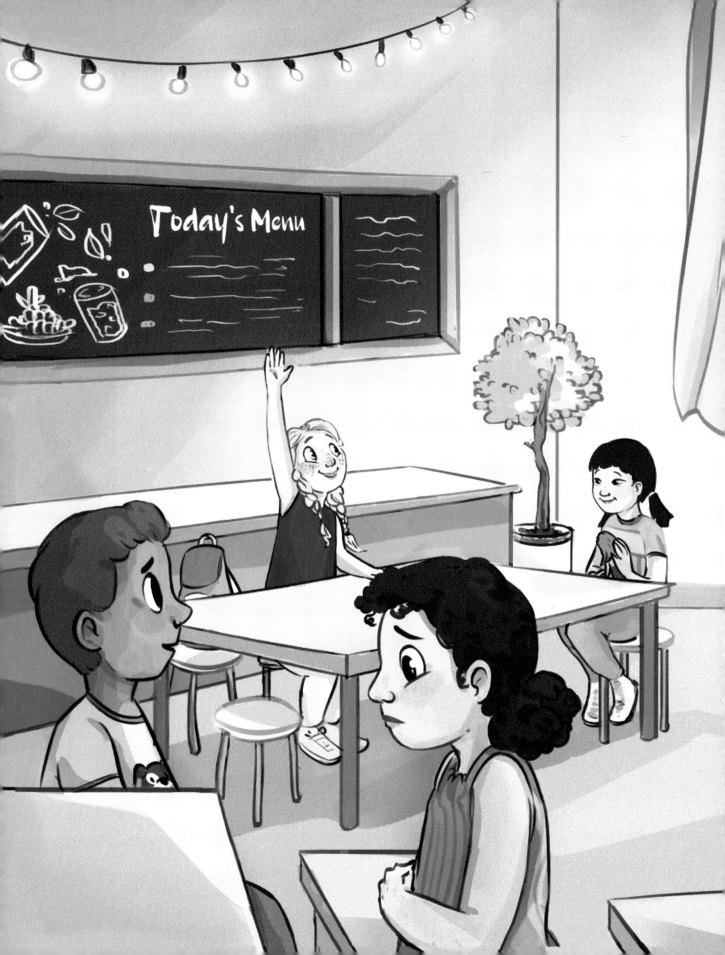

At snack time, a few of Janey's classmates
realised they had forgotten their snacks.

The teacher asked if anyone had spare.

Janey bravely raised her hand
and whispered, "I do."

Then she pulled out some extras
from her backpack.

Ten boxes of raisins, a small juice,
two oranges and, at the last minute,
two apples… just in case!

A girl sat next to Janey;
her backpack full.

She held her delicate hand out and
offered Janey a banana and some
chopped carrots.

"I'm Ella, shall we swap?
I brought lots of extras…"

"Just in case?" smiled Janey.
"Do you like raisins? I have loads!"

After snack time, Janey followed her new friends out to play.

She forgot her worries as they skipped, ran and jumped together.

She forgot about her backpack too, until it was time to go home.

Then she reached into it and
pulled out her wellie boots
and goggles.

After all, it looked like it
was about to rain, so,
just in case...

That night, Daddy made his famous macaroni cheese for dinner.

Janey felt calm, her words flowed with ease and her tummy was HUNGRY!
She asked for a GREAT BIG SLICE!

After dinner, Janey packed
her backpack for school the
next day, and took:

One bottle of water, a pencil case,
a cardigan...

And a few extras...
just in case!